Rancher Dick And The Little Gray Calf

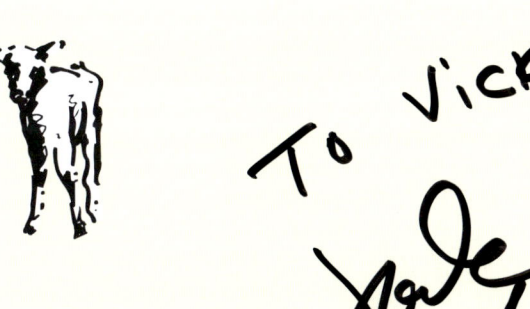

Jack Shabel

**Published by
Hara Publishing
P.O. Box 19732
Seattle, WA 98109
425-775-7868**

Copyright ©2003 by
Jack Shabel

All rights reserved

ISBN: 0-9710724-7-7

Library of Congress Catalog Card Number:
2003105815

Manufactured in Canada
10 9 8 7 6 5 4 3 2

No part of this book may be reproduced, stored in or introduced
into a retrieval system, or transmitted, in any form
or by any means (electronic, mechanical, photocopying, recording or otherwise)
without the prior written permission of the publisher.

Editor: Vicki McCown
Photographs: Jack Shabel
Cover Design: Scott Fisher
Book Design & Production: Scott Fisher

A number of people and one little heifer
helped in putting this book together.
I dedicate it to Dick & Margaret Rauth,
who educated me on cattle ranching;
to Anne, my wife and favorite children's librarian,
and to the little gray calf
who taught me about the will to survive.

In early spring, Rancher Dick and his wife move their pasture cows from the winter pasture to the calving pasture where their calves will be born.

Sometimes, calves show up early. Sometimes, they get left behind. That's what happened to the little gray calf. Her mother didn't want to take care of her, so Rancher Dick had to go out and pick her up and bring her to the ranch.

The first thing Rancher Dick
had to do was feed the
hungry little gray calf.
He put some milk from his
milk cow into a bottle
and fed the little
gray calf himself.

The little gray calf was happy with milk in her stomach. However, a rancher can't feed a calf with a bottle for very long. It takes too much time and there is too much work to do on a ranch.

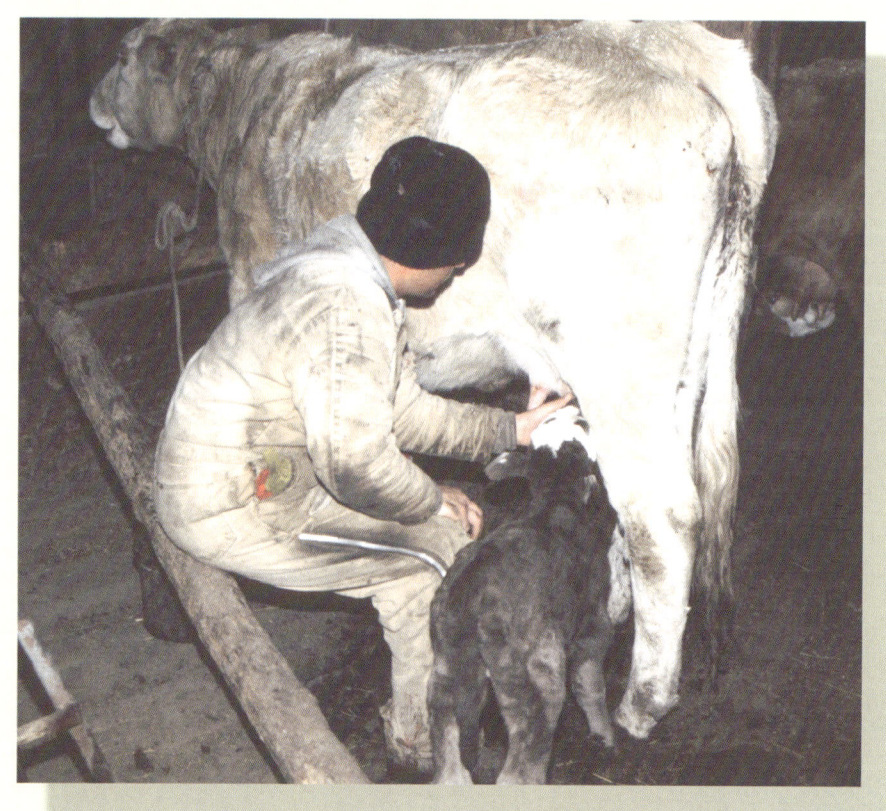

The next morning, ranch hand Josh tried to teach the calf how to get her breakfast from the milk cow all by herself.

But the little gray calf didn't understand and had to be fed with the bottle again. Rancher Dick and ranch hand Josh began to worry about the little gray calf.

The next morning Rancher Dick tried to teach the little gray calf again. But the little gray calf still didn't know what to do. Even Charlie the dog was worried about the little gray calf.

The future wasn't too bright for a little calf who couldn't feed herself.

Then, when no one was looking, the little gray calf figured out how to get milk all by herself. What a clever little calf.

But the place for a calf is in the pasture with all of the other calves and their mothers, not in the barn with milk cows, ranchers, and dogs.

That's why one day
Rancher Dick
rode out into the
calving pasture.

And he found a lonely pasture cow
who needed a little calf to adopt.
But first he had to fool the lonely cow.

When calves are first born, their mothers get to know and accept their calves by licking them.

Rancher Dick wanted the lonely pasture cow to lick the little gray calf, so he put powdered milk all over her. The lonely pasture cow thought the calf tasted delicious and she licked all the powdered milk off her.

After the little gray calf had been licked all over, the lonely cow decided to adopt her.

She and the little gray calf joined all the rest of the cows and calves in the pasture.

And it all happened because
Rancher Dick knew how
to help the little gray calf
and the lonely pasture cow.
What a clever rancher.

Glossary

Pasture – grassy area where the cattle feed.

Winter pasture – the pasture where the cattle spend their winter months. It is easy to reach from the ranch so that the rancher can check on the cattle every day and feed them with hay when snow covers the grass.

Calving pasture – the pasture where the cows spend the spring and where they deliver their calves. It is easy to reach from the ranch so that the rancher can check on the cows and calves twice a day. This pasture is the first to clear of snow and has the earliest grass.

Milk cow – a cow on the ranch that is kept to supply milk for orphaned calves, lambs and sometimes people. It is one of the milk breeds, such as a Guernsey or Holstein.

Pasture cow – a cow that is used for the breeding of beef cattle. The herd is kept in various pastures throughout the year. The pasture cows on Rancher Dick's spread are Black Angus.

Ranch hand – a person who is hired by the rancher to help with all of the work on the ranch.

Powdered milk – a fortified milk powder that is usually mixed with water. It is used to feed a calf that doesn't have a cow to nurse from.

Spread – the ranch property.

Jack Shabel is an electrical engineer by trade who left a management job in industry to pursue a career in photography. He observed the story of the little gray calf while taking photos in Alva, Wyoming, for a picture book about cattle ranching. This is his first book. He lives in Everett, Washington, with his wife Anne, an elementary school librarian.

Order Form

QTY.	Title	US Price	CN Price	Total
	Rancher Dick and The Little Gray Calf	$9.95	$13.95	
	Shipping and Handling Add $4.50 for orders in the US/Add $7.50 for Global Priority			
	Sales tax (WA state residents only, add 8.9%)			
	Total enclosed			

Telephone Orders:
Call **1-800-461-1931**
Have your VISA or MasterCard ready.

Method of Payment:

☐  Check or Money Order

☐  VISA

☐ MasterCard

INTL. Telephone Orders:
Toll free 1-877-250-5500
Have your credit card ready.

Fax Orders:
425-398-1380
Fill out this order form and fax.

Postal Orders:
Hara Publishing
P.O. Box 19732
Seattle, WA 98109

E-mail Orders:
harapub@foxinternet.net

Expiration Date: _____

Card #: _____

Signature: _____

Name _____
Address _____
City _____ State ____ Zip _____
Phone ( ) _____ Fax ( ) _____

Quantity discounts are available.
Call 425-398-3679 for more information.
Thank you for your order!